This book belongs to

_____

_____

for Vicki Churchill
without whom none of these stories would have been possible
C.F.

STERLING and the distinctive Sterling logo are registered trademarks of Sterling Publishing Co., Inc.

Library of Congress Cataloging in Publication Data Available

2 4 6 8 10 9 7 5 3 1

Published in 2008 by Sterling Publishing Co., Inc.
387 Park Avenue South, New York, NY 10016
First published in this edition in Great Britain in 2008 by
Gullane Children's Books
185 Fleet Street, London, EC4A 2HS
www.gullanebooks.com

Sometimes I Like to Curl up in a Ball
Text © Vicki Churchill 2001
Illustrations © Charles Fuge 2001

Found You, Little Wombat!
Text © Angela McAllister 2003
Illustrations © Charles Fuge 2003

Swim, Little Wombat, Swim!
Text and Illustrations © Charles Fuge 2005

Where To, Little Wombat?
Text and Illustrations © Charles Fuge 2006

Distributed in Canada by Sterling Publishing
C/o Canadian Manda Group, 165 Dufferin St. Toronto, Ontario, Canada M6K 3H6

Sterling ISBN 978-1-4027-6322-9

The Adventures of
Little Wombat

illustrated by Charles Fuge

STERLING

New York / London
www.sterlingpublishing.com/kids

The Adventures of
Little Wombat

CONTENTS

Sometimes I Like to Curl up in a Ball

written by Vicki Churchill

illustrated by Charles Fuge

Sometimes I like
to curl up in a ball,
So no one can see me
because I'm so small.

Sometimes I like to jump
high as I can,

To see how much
noise I can make
when I land.

Sometimes I like to just
walk round and round,

I pigeon step, pigeon step, till I fall down.

Sometimes
I like to
stand
still as
a tree,

And watch
everyone
rush around
about me.

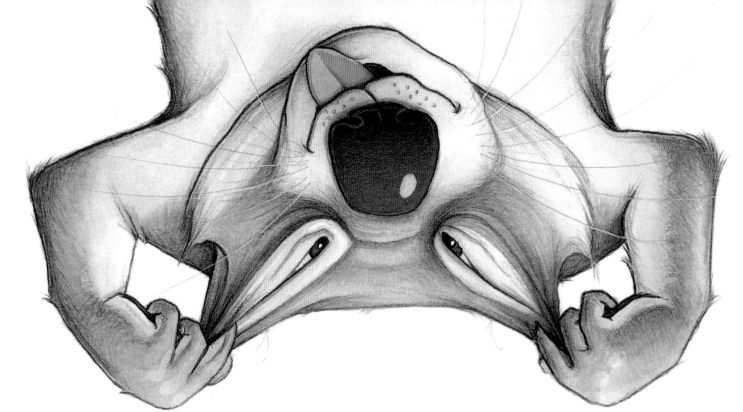

Sometimes I like to
poke out my tongue,

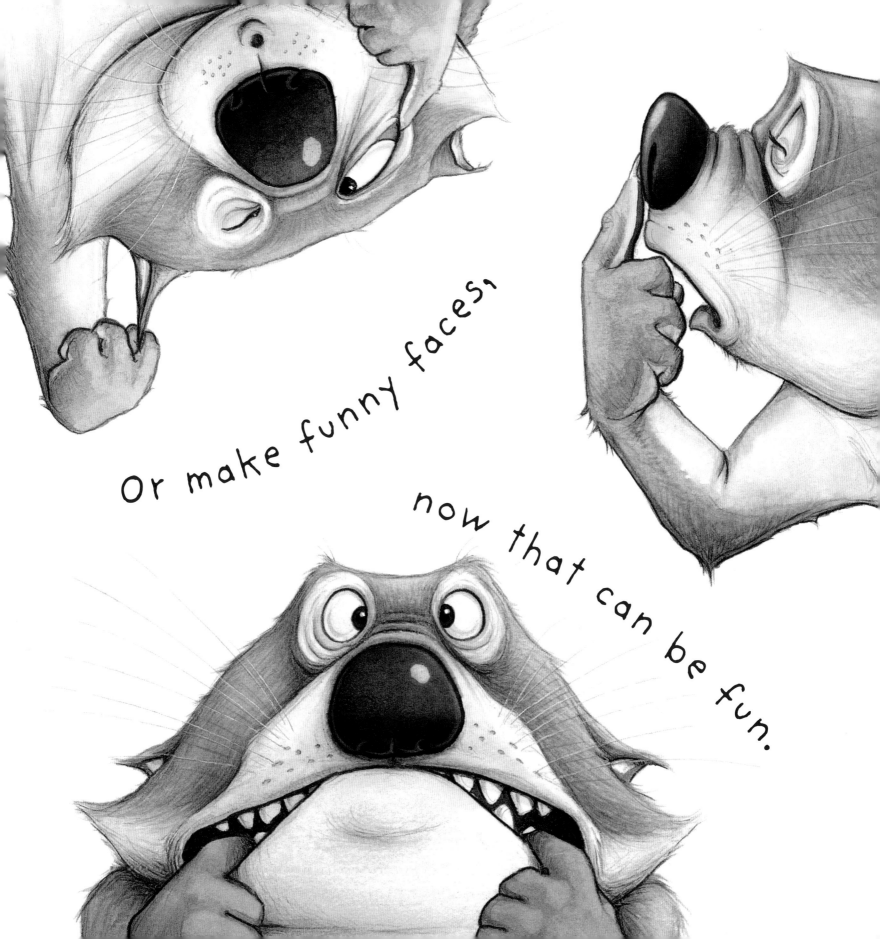

Or make funny faces,

now that can be fun.

Sometimes I like to get
in a real mess,

With mud on my feet and
my hands and my chest.

Sometimes I like to run
ever so fast,

I sometimes come first,
but I sometimes come last.

But when the day ends
and the sun starts to fall,
Then I do what I do best of all.
I find somewhere soft,
somewhere cozy and small...

...And that's where I like to curl up in a ball.

Found You, Little Wombat!

written by Angela McAllister
illustrated by Charles Fuge

Little Wombat was playing hide-and-seek with Rabbit and Koala.

"Found you!" said Koala.

"Now it's your turn to seek, Little Wombat!"
said Rabbit.

Rabbit and Koala hid, and
so did Little Wombat.

They waited and waited . . .
and tried to keep very quiet.
So did Little Wombat!

"Let's start again!" said Koala with a chuckle. "You have to count to ten and then come and find us." Little Wombat shut his eyes.
"Two, TEN!"

"No, no! Count ten flowers before you come and find us," called Rabbit and Koala, as they ran away to hide.

"One . . ." counted Little Wombat.
But he soon became distracted and
began to look around.

Little Wombat wandered over a hill to see what was on the other side . . .

He didn't notice a cloud
creep in front of the sun.
He didn't notice the sky turn gray.
He didn't notice the wind
shake the trees.

He suddenly remembered that Rabbit and Koala were hiding. "Ten! I'm coming!" he shouted.

But where was Koala?
Where was Rabbit?
Little Wombat felt all alone.
"Where am I?" he asked.

DRIP . . . DRIP.
    Raindrops started to fall
        from a small, dark cloud.

DRIP . . . DRIP.
    Teardrops started to fall
        from a small, lost wombat.

But the sun didn't hide
for long. And neither did
Little Wombat.
"Hmm, that's a very
wobbly toadstool . . .

. . . found you!" said Mom.
"What a clever umbrella!"

"Let's splash in the puddles on the way home," said Rabbit. So Little Wombat jumped and made the biggest, happiest splash of all.

Swim, Little Wombat, Swim!

by Charles Fuge

Little Wombat was looking for apples.
"Hello," said a funny squeaky voice.
Wombat spun around.
"Hello! I'm Wombat, who are you?"
"I'm Platypus," said a funny, fuzzy face.

Then, with a funny, shuffly walk, Platypus waddled to the pond and disappeared

"PLA-TY-PUS!" Little Wombat
giggled. "PLA-TY-PUS!"

He tried to waddle too. He giggled and
waddled, shuffled and chuckled nearer and
nearer to the water's edge . . .

KER-SPLASH!

Little Wombat sank like a stone.

In a flash, Platypus
darted towards him.

Before he knew it, Wombat was at the surface . . .

. . . and safely out of the water.
"Thank you, Platypus," he spluttered. He
wished he hadn't laughed at his new friend.
"How did you learn to swim like that?"
"It's easy!" Platypus smiled.
"I'll teach you!"

First Little Wombat had to hold onto the edge and kick his legs as hard as he could.

Then he used a log as a float, and he splashed all around the pond.

He splashed and kicked until he was worn out.
"Time for lunch!" said Platypus.

Little Wombat munched on juicy red apples and Platypus munched on a handful of shrimps.

"Never swim on a full tummy," said Platypus. So they snoozed in the shade for an hour.

That afternoon, Little Wombat
learned to paddle like a dog . . .

and dive like a frog!

Then through all the splashing,
Little Wombat heard his
name being called.

Rabbit and Koala had come to see
what he had been doing all day.
Little Wombat beamed.
"PLATYPUS taught me to swim!
Come on, Platypus, let's have a race."

A-AT,
WOM-BA-AT!"
Koala and Rabbit
cheered him on.

"No ... not Wombat ..." Little Wombat grinned at his new friend,

"WOM-BATYPUS!"

Where To, Little Wombat?

by Charles Fuge

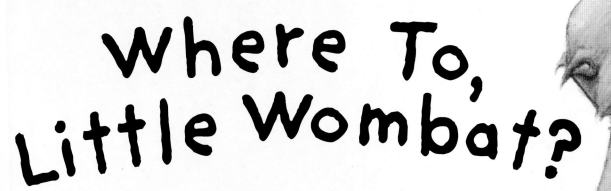

Little Wombat's mom was spring-cleaning the burrow. "I wish we could live somewhere more exciting," grumbled Little Wombat. "I'm bored of burrows."

"Well then," said Mom. "Why don't you go and see if you can find somewhere better?" She was very busy.

Koala was up his gum tree eating leaves. "Can I live with you?" asked Little Wombat.

Koala thought it was a great idea...

But wombats aren't built to climb trees!

Frog was resting on
his favorite lily pad.

"Can I live with you?"
asked Little Wombat.
Frog thought it was a
fantastic idea...

But wombats are too
heavy to walk on lily pads!

Mole was digging new tunnels as usual.
"Can I live with you?" asked Little Wombat.

Mole thought it was
a marvelous idea . . .

But wombats are much
bigger than moles!

Turtle was asleep inside his shell.
"No room here!"

But the ants knew
of a great big
nest nearby.

Little Wombat was just making
himself comfortable . . .

. . . when angry Mrs. Emu appeared
and shooed him away.

Little Wombat arrived at the burrow looking sorry for himself.

"Home so soon?" asked Mom kindly.

"Welcome back to the burrow," she said.
"Ours is nice and tidy now, with *plenty* of room!"
That gave Little Wombat a wonderful idea.
The burrow did have plenty of room . . .

. . . for a sleepover with all his friends!